COOKIES AND CONDOLENCES

CHRISTIAN COZY MYSTERY

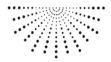

DONNA DOYLE

© 2019 PUREREAD LTD

PUREREAD.COM

CONTENTS

INTRODUCTION

A PERSONAL WORD FROM PUREREAD

 Dear reader,

Do you love a good mystery? So do we! Nothing is more pleasing than a page turner that keeps you guessing until the very last page.

In our Christian cozy mysteries you can be certain that there won't be any gruesome or gory scenes, swearing or anything else upsetting, just good clean fun as you unravel the mystery together with our marvelous characters.

Thank you for choosing PureRead!

To find out more about PureRead mysteries and receive new release information and other goodies from Donna Doyle go to our website PureRead.com/donnadoyle

* * *

Enjoy The Story!

A PINCH OF EXCITEMENT

S ammy Baker pushed open the door of the plush law office in downtown Sunny Cove, her stomach swirling anxiously. She'd received a call from Rob Hewitt earlier that morning, and he'd refused to give her any details over the phone. "I think it's much better if we talk about it in person."

That hadn't sounded good. When Sammy had gone to him just over a month ago, she didn't really think this project was going to go anywhere. If he had news and he wouldn't say it over the phone, then he was trying to let her down gently. Sammy assured herself that it would be all right. Just because she couldn't get it done this way didn't mean that was the end of it. There would be other opportunities.

Stacey, Rob's secretary, barely looked up from her cell phone as Sammy walked into the lobby. "He said you can go right in," she mumbled.

"Thanks." Sammy had to wonder why Rob wasted his money on an employee who did nothing but play games or text on her cell, but that wasn't really any of her business.

Rob, the most popular jock back when the two of them had gone to Sunny Cove High School together, was behind his massive oak desk as usual. The bank of windows behind him showed the drizzly rain that had been plaguing the town for the last few days, and they didn't make the grim look on his face any more cheerful. "Have a seat," he said, gesturing at the leather chair in front of his desk.

Sammy sat, already feeling dejected. "I guess it didn't go over well, did it?"

The lawyer sat back, running his hand over his chin and meeting Sammy's eyes with his own bright green ones. "You know, starting up a business like this isn't a very easy thing to do. It's going to take a lot of money, but it's not the kind of thing that really *makes* money."

"I know. I knew that going in, but I just really

thought it was worth trying. Austin has been so cagey over the winter with nothing to do. I was hoping I could get him some jobs shoveling snow, but we just haven't had that much this year. You were right with what you'd told me before, that I couldn't put it all on my shoulders. I love volunteering, and I love seeing how happy Austin is when he completes a job, but there just isn't enough time in the day to get it all done." Sammy knew she shouldn't feel so dejected. She and Rob had done what they could.

Rob smiled. "Fortunately, the grant committee isn't concerned about how much money we'll make."

"What?" Sammy lifted her head and felt her mouth drop open. "What are you telling me?"

His smile increased. "Ever since you came to me and asked if Austin could pick up trash outside my building, I've been trying to think of ways we could truly help him. I really thought this grant and the business we talked about would be the answer, but I admit I was a little nervous about whether or not we would get approved. It turns out we did, and I can happily tell you that Sunny Cove Services is going to become a real thing."

Sammy was out of her seat, her fists in the air and a grin on her face. "That's so exciting! Praise the Lord! I can't believe this!" She'd been shocked that Rob was so willing to help her find a long-term solution for Austin and people like him. Sunny Cove Services would act as a contracting company that would hire out disabled adults looking for work. The types of work they would do at first would be very simple, but as the company was built up and more equipment was acquired, they would be able to do assembly projects and shred documents.

"You'd better believe it, and you'd also better believe that we have a lot to do to get this place up and running."

"Where do we start?" Sammy was so excited she couldn't even remember what came next.

"The first thing we need is a place to open this business. I have a place in mind, and if you have the time I'd love for you to come look at it with me."

"Absolutely!" Sammy's heart was thundering in her chest as all the dreams she had for Sunny Cove Services came swirling to the forefront of her mind. There were so many things she knew Austin would be capable of if he just had the right training and someone to guide him. It thrilled her even more to know they would be helping people like him all through their area.

Rob led the way out to his car, a sleek black luxury sedan, and opened the passenger door for her. "I took the liberty of making an appointment to see this place, because I figured you'd be just as excited as I am."

"Is it going to be big enough?" The two of them had discussed the fact that they would need plenty of space to allow room for work area and supplies. That had been one of Sammy's main concerns, since many of the buildings in Sunny Cove were smaller, older places.

"I think so. Its downtown, so nobody should have a problem finding it or getting to it. The best part is that it's available immediately." Rob pulled up next to the Stargazer Theater.

"What are we doing here?" Sammy was instantly confused. She looked around, expecting one of the nearby downtown building to have a "For Rent" sign on it that she'd missed.

"Come on in and you'll see."

The theater didn't open until later in the evening during the week, but the front door swung wide and a tall brunette welcomed them. "Rob! It's so good to see you!"

"Sammy, I think you know Sonya McTavish. She was a few years ahead of us in high school."

"Oh, Robbie. You don't have to point *that* out. Come on in."

Rob gave Sammy an innocent shrug and gestured for her to precede him.

"I can't tell you how happy I am that you called," Sonya said as she sauntered across the patterned carpet in the lobby. "I was happy to take over the theater after Daddy went to jail, but it's always bothered me that I have this big, useless space." She opened a door off to the left.

Sammy understood what was going on even before she went inside. She'd been in this part of the Stargazer only once before, when she'd helped uncover an underground gambling den that Sonya's dad had been running in secret. The crap tables, roulette wheels, and slot machines had been removed, leaving only a large space with tall ceilings.

"It was the first place that came to mind. Does this

section of the building have its own outside access?" Rob stood in the center of the room, turning slowly as he examined it.

"Right over there. It hasn't been used for as long as I can remember, so the lock might need to be replaced."

Rob put his chin in his hand. "Not a problem. And do you have any issue with some remodeling? I'm thinking we pull out the old carpet and put down linoleum, replace the paneling with drywall, and get some better lighting in here. Really make it look professional, you know?"

"Certainly."

"It looks like this old bathroom could easily be converted into a larger one with stalls," Sammy called as she explored the space, the excitement building inside her once again. "And there would be plenty of room for some big shredders and some nice, spacious work tables." It was hard to see past the red carpet with gold swirls, but the longer they spent here the more she could see this working.

Sonya slid her catlike eyes from Rob to Sammy and back again and smiled. "Sounds like you two have quite an idea brewing here."

"We do, and the grant money will be in shortly. We want to get started as soon as possible."

Sammy didn't think she'd seen Rob look that happy since he made the winning play for the football championship their senior year. He'd seemed the most unlikely person to get involved in a project like this, but Sammy was beginning to understand that he wasn't the selfish, materialistic person she'd known back in school.

Sonya shrugged. "Well, you're the lawyer. Draw up a contract and I'll sign it. I don't expect much in rent. I'm sure there's some sort of write-off for housing a non-profit under your roof, and I'd much rather see something good come of the space." She frowned slightly at an old sconce on the wall that had been painted a very tacky shade of gold. "You know where to find me if you need me." She slunk out the door, leaving the two of them alone.

Sammy turned to Rob, unable to stop the grin that had completely taken over her face. "Well, what do you think? Do we need to look anywhere else?"

Rob shook his head. "We can if you want to, but I don't imagine any other space will be more ideal. We won't make a ton of noise, but even if we do there's extra soundproofing in the walls to keep the theater goers from hearing us. It'll take some remodeling, but I imagine any place would. I say we jump on it before Sonya changes her mind and brings in something that'll make her a lot more money."

"Great! Let's do it!"

"Sounds good to me, but there are a few more things we need to figure out."

Sammy was so ready to dive headfirst into this venture, and it was hard to slow down and make sure it was all done the right way. "Okay. What did you have in mind?"

"First of all, we need a manager. You can't run this place and still work at the diner, and you mentioned that you didn't want to leave Helen."

"I really don't." Sammy gave a thought for her boss, who'd been so kind to give her both a job and an apartment when she'd moved back to Sunny Cove from New York. Sammy had quickly proven her baking skills and was currently selling her goods out of the diner as well as acting as a waitress, dishwasher, and anything else Helen needed. It was a nice arrangement between the two of them, and Sammy couldn't leave it.

"How do you feel about letting me hire a manager? I've got a lot of experience in hiring people."

Sammy started to nod her enthusiasm, but she stopped as soon as she remembered what Rob's secretary was like. "We could always make it a joint effort."

"Oh, I get it," Rob said with a laugh. "If you're worried about Stacey, you can forget about it. My full-time secretary is pregnant and was put on bed rest. Stacey is my cousin, and she's just filling in until Miranda gets back."

A sense of relief fell over Sammy. "I'm sorry. I didn't mean to get into your business."

"No, it's completely fine. I've had lots of complaints about Stacey, so you're not the first to notice she's less than attentive. I wish I'd never hired her, but she needed a job and I owed my aunt a favor. I'm perfectly happy to let you approve the final candidate."

Sammy felt a little silly for judging him like that. It wasn't the Christian thing to do. "No, that's okay. You probably know a lot more about this kind of thing than I do."

"It'll take some time to find the right person, but in

the meantime we need a contractor to get this place fixed up. You know anybody?"

"Not offhand, but I'm happy to find one if you're going to locate a manager for us. Deal?" Sammy extended her hand.

Rob smiled and shook it. "Deal, partner."

2

A TEASPOON OF PLANNING

"**O**kay, you see how the tops of the cookies have just started to brown a little bit? That means they're done. Do you want to pull them out yourself?"

Austin nodded enthusiastically and reached into the oven.

"Wait, wait! You need an oven mitt!" Sammy snatched one off the counter and handed it to him.

His dark eyes fell to the floor. "I'm sorry. I messed up again."

"Don't you dare think about it that way!" Sammy rubbed his arm affectionately. After spending so much time with Austin, she was starting to feel a real sense of responsibility for him. His Uncle Mitch was his guardian, but the old man didn't have the time, patience, or energy to teach him what he needed to know. "I just don't want you to get hurt. And that's exactly why you're here doing this with me instead of doing it on your own. Now, just put on the oven mitts and then you can take the cookies out. Then I'll show you how to move them to a wire rack to cool."

"My favorite cookies are the ones with sprinkles," Austin said as he carefully removed the hot pan from the oven. "Can we put sprinkles on them?"

Sammy smiled patiently. "We were going to put icing on these cookies, remember? But we can put sprinkles on the next batch."

"You mean we can make more?"

"Of course. I always need lots of baked goods to keep the diner stocked, so it won't hurt to make a few extras." Sammy had been on a real cookie kick lately, churning out chocolate chip, oatmeal, and sugar cookies by the panful. Fortunately, they'd been selling just as well as her other goodies. Helen had warned her that it would be difficult to let Austin into the kitchen to help, but Sammy was determined to try. There weren't any other jobs she had for him at the moment, and it was best to keep him busy so he didn't get himself into trouble.

"Will you teach me how to make a cake? Bakeries in Germany sold birthday cakes in the 1400s." Austin had a knack for memorizing random facts he heard on documentaries that he watched with his uncle, and he seemed to enjoy sharing those facts with others.

"Is that so?" Sammy fetched a spatula from a drawer and handed it to him. "I'm sure we can make a cake sometime." The idea got her mind churning once again. She hadn't been able to stop thinking about the upcoming Sunny Cove Services ever since her meeting with Rob the day before, and her project notebook on the subject was quickly filling up.

"Sammy! There's someone here to see you!" Helen called through the kitchen door.

"Be right there!" She turned to Austin, who looked disappointed that she had to go. "Don't you give me that puppy dog look! We'll have plenty more chances to bake, and I'll make sure I set some of these cookies aside for you to take home once they've cooled. Here, why don't you go sit down with a sandwich and take a break?"

Austin did as he was told, giving only one longing

glance at the cookies before heading into the dining room with his sandwich.

Just Like Grandma's was bustling with customers for a midweek afternoon, a sight that made Sammy's heart happy. She liked to know that Helen was still getting such good business, even if Sammy's job here wasn't exactly how the older woman had probably envisioned it when she'd hired her. Helen needed someone with baking and waitressing skills, but Sammy spent far more time with the oven than she did on the floor. The fact that she was selling boxes and bags of her rolls, buns, breads, cookies, and cakes from a table in the back corner probably didn't help, but Helen didn't seem to mind.

Sammy felt it only made matters worse that she was taking time out of her day to interview contractors, but Helen had been very generous about that as well as soon as she knew what Sammy had up her sleeve. "You go right ahead, dear. The world won't stop just because you sat down for a minute, and the good Lord knows we need a place like that around here."

The man waiting for her was dressed simply in a worn polo and khakis, and he carried a plain manila file folder in one hand. He was an older man with a fringe of a gray beard around his jaw line, and he shook her hand warmly. "I'm Harold Woodland."

"It's so nice to meet you, Mr. Woodland. Let's find a place to sit down." Sammy guided the contractor to an empty table, eager to see what he had to say about the project. "Did you get a chance to go look at the space?"

"Sonya was kind enough to let me in. It's definitely going to need some work to get it all shaped up, but I think we can make it happen within your timeline."

"Wonderful to hear!" Sammy sat forward as he pulled a few papers out of the file folder. "I can't tell you how excited I am about opening this place up."

Mr. Woodland gave her a small smile. "Word is traveling fast about it, too. When you called and asked me to do a bid, I'd already heard a few rumors about what you are doing."

"Oh, really? I hope they were all good." Sammy should've known she couldn't keep this under wraps for long. The people of Sunny Cove were just like the residents of any other small town in America. They loved to gossip.

"Of course! Anyplace that'll give people jobs is a good thing, and you're really fulfilling a need with this. I have a cousin who'll be interested in coming to work for you."

"Well, not for *me*, exactly," Sammy corrected gently. "It's not something I'm doing for myself. We're setting it up as a non-profit organization. We'll be hiring someone to manage the place, and I'll still work here." She didn't quite understand all the legalities of it, but Rob was handling that end of things.

"I see. Here's what I've got so far. I understand there might be some adjustments you need to make, and there'll probably be some adjustments on our end as well, but this should give you at least a general idea." He handed her several pieces of paper, reaching across the table to circle the total cost on the bid sheet.

Sammy was shocked at the low number, and she tried not to let it show on her face. "Okay. We might be able to work with that. I'm going to collect bids from several contractors before we make our final decision. I'm sure you understand."

"Of course. You do what you need to do. But keep in mind that I'm local, and I use all local workers as well. I don't bring in people from out of state just because they're cheaper. You hear things in my line of work, and I'm sure you do as well. It helps you know just what kind of people you're dealing with."

Sammy couldn't deny that she'd heard her fair share of rumors since she'd come back to Sunny Cove, and most of them had been overheard while she was waiting tables. She never meant to eavesdrop, but it was impossible to avoid when you were surrounded by people all day. "I suppose that's true."

I have a few references here for you, if you'd like them." He handed her another piece of paper.

Appreciating how professional it all seemed, Sammy added the references to the pile. "Thank you. I'll be sure to let you know if we decide to go with you."

"I have no doubt that there are a lot of other contractors in the running for this," he admitted, folding his hands humbly on the table. "This time of year, people aren't interested in fixing up their homes, and it's too wet outside to think of building something new. I know the competition is steep, but I can promise you all my best work."

They shook hands, and Mr. Woodland headed out the door.

"What do you think?" asked a voice over her shoulder.

Startled, Sammy swiveled in her seat to find Helen leaning over the back of the booth. "Oh! Well, he had everything put together for me, and he does have a very reasonable price."

"Well, price isn't everything, but I know that's certainly a lot of it. And there are a lot of people in this little old town looking for work. What does the Hewitt boy think about all this?" Helen tossed her thick, gray braid over her shoulder.

"He's taking care of the management, and I'm taking care of the contractor. I'll have him look over the bid for whoever we go with, but it's mostly up to me." Sammy flushed a little at the knowledge that someone trusted her with such a big decision. Before she'd moved back to Sunny Cove, back when she'd still been with her ex, Greg had always treated her as though she wasn't smart enough to make even the tiniest choices about their lives. Now, she was helping to start a completely new company.

"I have to be honest with you. I have one major concern about this enterprise." Helen's pale eyes watched her seriously. "I know you're a hard worker, Sammy. It's one of the things I love about you. But I don't want to see you get burned out. If you're burning the candle at both ends, you're liable to melt in the middle."

Sammy smiled up at her boss, appreciating that she

cared about her so much. "I'll be all right. Oh, and I wanted to tell you about a great idea I had earlier. Austin has really enjoyed getting baking lessons from me. Once we get Sunny Cove Services up and running, I thought I could go over there once a week or so to teach cooking skills. I've heard of other organizations similar to ours that not only give employment opportunities but help with basic life skills as well."

Helen smiled fondly. "Like I said, dear, burning the candle at both ends. And I hate to encourage it, but we're getting pretty backed up. Do you think you could help me out on the floor for a little while?"

"Absolutely!" Sammy hopped to her feet, adjusted her apron, and began checking on the tables.

"Ah, Sammy. I'm glad to see you," said an older woman at the table in the front corner near the window. "I wondered if you had time to sit down and chat with me." Julia Richardson was rumored to be one of the wealthiest people in town, although nobody really knew how much money she had. At the very least, she had plenty of jewelry, and she wore it no matter the occasion. Today, her pearl earrings and necklace picked up what little sunlight came through the gloomy clouds and glowed against her deep purple sweater.

"Not really, Mrs. Richardson. Helen needs me."

"Well then I won't bother you for very long. I saw you talking to that Harold Woodland a few minutes ago. You aren't considering using his services for anything are you?"

Sammy pursed her lips. The line between gossip and conversation was a thin one, and while she was certainly free to talk about her own business, it made her hesitate when the subject turned to someone else involved. "You might've heard that I'm working on starting up a—"

"Oh, yes, yes, darling. I know all about it. It's a grand, wonderful thing I'm sure. But what you really need to know right now is that Mr. Woodland is a scam artist. He remodeled my guest bathroom, or at least that's what I hired him to do. He made a complete mess of the place! It had been outdated, sure, but at least it still worked!"

"I'm, um, I'm sorry to hear that." Sammy shoved her hands in the pocket of her apron, feeling as though she'd been put on the spot. "I'll be sure to check the references of anyone we choose to go with."

"And do you really think those contractors will be honest about that? They'll give you the names of their friends and family, or some schmuck they've paid off to say they did a great job! Honey, sometimes I think you're just too sweet for this world." She shook her head and clucked her tongue against the roof of her mouth.

Unsure of whether to take that as a compliment or an insult, Sammy just smiled. "Thanks for the advice, Mrs. Richardson. I'll be sure to keep it in mind."

"You do that. And you watch that Rob Hewitt, as well. You can't trust a lawyer, no matter how handsome he is." Julia pointed a ringed finger at Sammy and narrowed her eyes.

Sammy couldn't imagine that Rob was anyone who needed to be watched, but she wasn't about to get into an argument with a customer over something so arbitrary. "Can I get you anything else?"

The older woman pressed her bright red lips together, clamping them down on whatever else she might have a mind to say. "I've been eyeing that chocolate silk pie you put on the counter earlier. I'll take a slice of that and a check."

"Coming right up." As Sammy continued her work, she thought a lot about what Mrs. Richardson had said. How would she know the right person for the job?

3

HALF A CUP OF HARD WORK

Now that the rental agreement had been finalized, Sonya McTavish had given Rob and Sammy each a key to the big space adjacent to the Stargazer. Early on Thursday morning before she started work at Just Like Grandma's, Sammy used hers in the rusty lock on the outside door and let herself in. She juggled a carafe of coffee under one arm, set it down on an old blackjack table that had been left behind, and then returned to her Toyota for a box of fresh doughnuts.

She was looking forward to seeing what Harold Woodland would do with the place. It certainly didn't look anything like a place where disabled adults could be employed, not unless they wanted to learn how to deal cards, but she knew there was a lot of potential. She walked in a slow circle around the perimeter, hoping that all her dreams would be a reality soon enough. It would be a long process, and things wouldn't happen instantly, but she really hoped she could help Austin and others with this place.

"Knock, knock!"

Sammy turned around, expecting to see Harold Woodland, but a different familiar face was peeking in the door. "Mr. Herzog, what are you doing here?"

The land developer strode in the room. He was an incredibly tall man, and Sammy was fairly certain all his suits had to be custom made to fit him as well as they did. He looked around, taking in the ancient paneling and the horrid carpet. "So, this is the place, huh?"

"I take it you already know what we're trying to do here." Everyone else did, so it was no surprise that a business man like Andrew would know as well.

"I do, and may I say I think it's a great idea. There'll be a lot of people who will benefit." He gave a curt but approving nod.

"I'm hoping so," Sammy said with a smile. "I've been looking for a way to help the community ever since I moved back here. I think this is a good way to do it."

"So do I," Mr. Herzog said, nodding again, "but I'm not sure you're going about it right."

This surprised her. "Oh? And why is that?"

"Well, it's going to take an awful lot of money to turn this place around. I'm sure right now you're just thinking about simple things, like replacing the wall and floor coverings, maybe upgrading the bathroom."

"Yes, that's definitely in the plan."

Andrew sighed and scratched the back of his head. "But you don't really know what you're going to run into once you remove this old paneling. What if there's asbestos in the walls? Or termite damage? What if you have to replace the structure of the walls as well as the paneling? And there's no telling what's under this floor." He frowned down at the carpet and bounced on one foot, testing it out.

"I'm pretty sure it's just concrete," she replied, a small smile on her face. She knew where he was going with this.

"Still, you're going to put an awful lot of money into a place that you're *renting*. That's not a very good business plan, long-term. What happens if Sonya sells the theater, and the new owner doesn't want to rent to you guys anymore? These things happen, you know. It'd be a much better idea if you started over, brand new. I've got plans for a building I'd be happy to show you."

"If these are the same plans you tried to sell me for the restaurant, I'm not interested." Mr. Herzog wasn't always well-liked in the community due to his ideas about tearing down old buildings and erecting new ones in their place, but Sammy didn't really blame him. That was his job. "Even if it's a new plan, we just can't afford it. We're starting this up on a small government grant, and the rent here is low. Buying land and a new building is more of an investment than we can make right now, even if we wanted to."

Mr. Herzog shrugged. "I guess I can see that. I just hate to see you guys run into any problems, especially with what you're trying to do here."

"We'll be all right. I've got a contractor coming in today to get started, and we should be up and running within a month or two."

"Yeah, about that…" Andrew pressed his thumb and finger against his chin, looking serious.

"Yes?"

"I heard you're using Harold Woodland."

"This is true," she answered hesitantly. It hadn't been an easy decision to make. Some contractors promised the fastest turnaround, and others had promised the best quality materials. Mr. Woodland seemed to be the best of all worlds, and the price was low. Rob had agreed with her when she'd gone to him for his opinion.

"Did you know that he works out of his home?"

Sammy shook her head. "I didn't know that, but I'm not sure why it matters."

"It's incredibly unprofessional, to start with. I mean, the guy is probably drafting up plans on his kitchen table."

"Mr. Herzog, please. I don't care if he draws them on a napkin as long as he understands what I need. And he really seems to." Of all the contractors she'd interviewed, Mr. Woodland seemed the most down-to-earth. She just had a good feeling about him, but she didn't imagine that was the kind of thing Andrew would understand.

He held up his hands, palms out. "Okay, okay. But I've heard other bad things about him, too. Shoddy work, shoddy workers, things like that."

"And have you witnessed any of this firsthand?" Sammy challenged.

His shoulders slumped slightly in his blazer. "No, I suppose not. I just don't want to see you and Mr. Hewitt get taken advantage of."

"I appreciate that, but I've already hired him." And Mr. Woodland had seemed very excited when she'd called and given him the good news.

"Okay, I can respect that. But if things go south, remember that I've got a good guy I use all the time. The name of the company is Jackson and Sons. They're very modern, very competent. They're fully licensed and insured, which is more than I can say for most of the other guys around here."

"Aren't they based out of Oak Hills?" Sammy had made sure she'd only talked to contractors based out of Sunny Cove in an effort to keep things as local as possible. This new business was going to benefit her friends and neighbors as much as possible.

"They are, and they've got a state-of-the-art office with all the latest software. When they give you a bid, they don't miss a single nail."

"I really do appreciate the advice, but Mr. Woodland is on his way here right now. I can't and won't just change my mind at the last minute." It wouldn't be the right thing to do, and this Jackson and Sons that Mr. Herzog recommended sounded very expensive.

"Suit yourself, but don't say I didn't warn you."

"Would you like a cup of coffee or a doughnut?" She'd brought the goodies for Harold and his crew, but she could always bring more if there wasn't enough. Besides, Sammy's hospitality was hard to repress.

He waved away the offer. "Thanks, but no thanks. I have some gourmet stuff in the car. I'll see you around, Ms. Baker."

As he made his way out the door, Mr. Woodland came in. He wore a similar outfit to the one she'd seen him in at the diner. This polo was a faded orange instead of green, and there was a small spot of paint on the knee of his khakis. "Good morning, Sammy!"

"Good morning! I brought some doughnuts and coffee for you guys." She gestured to the table. "Feel free to help yourselves."

"Thank you. That's very kind. I'm sure they won't mind a little caffeine to keep things rolling along, right boys?" He smiled at his crewmen as they filed in the door carrying toolboxes and ladders. They smiled back or nodded, but they were mostly interested in looking around at the space that would become Sunny Cove Services. "We'll get started with the demolition today. I have a dumpster on order that should arrive later on this afternoon. I made sure to just get a small one so it wouldn't be in the way for Miss McTavish."

"Is there anything you need from me? I do need to get to the diner soon." She wanted very badly to stick around and watch the work, or even jump in and help. Sammy had wielded a hammer a time or two, and it would be fun to be part of the renovations. Still, she knew she had an obligation to Helen, and she'd been dropping the ball a lot lately.

"No, not really. Is there a way I can lock up when we're done?"

"Oh, I hadn't thought about that!" Sammy fished the key out of her pocket and handed it over. She could get another one from Sonya or borrow Rob's if need be. "Here you go. That way you can lock up when you're done, and you can get here however early you want to in the mornings."

Just then, the door opened and admitted a muscular man with dark hair and wild eyes. Sammy was facing the door, so she saw him right away, but Mr. Woodland didn't miss the creak of the rusty old door. He turned on his heel and called out. "Garrett! How many times do I have to tell you to show up on time? You make all the rest of us look bad! Excuse me, Sammy." Harold strode across the room to talk to his worker.

Sammy's phone rang in her back pocket, which seemed to be good timing. "Hello?"

"Hi, Ms. Baker. It's Ken Lowry. I just wanted to check with you and see if you'd had a chance to go over my bid."

She pressed her palm against her forehead, realizing she'd forgotten to call all the contractors that *didn't* get the job. "I'm so sorry. I meant to call you yesterday. We've decided to go with someone else."

"Can I ask who?"

Once again, Sammy warred with herself on what to say. It wasn't really anyone else's business, but she didn't want anyone to think she was trying to keep it a secret, either. "Harold Woodland. He's starting this morning."

"Are you kidding me? You actually hired that guy?"

Sammy pulled in a deep breath and let it out slowly.

She had been so excited to get this project started, but now she was getting yelled at over the phone. That wasn't how she hoped her day would go. "I did, not that it's any of your business."

"Oh, but it will be when I have to come in and finish up his shoddy work. I know Woodland, and I know the kind of work he does. He'll either leave it half-done and you'll have to hire someone else, or he'll make it look like its finished and you won't discover the truth until later. Guys like him are just out to make a quick buck, and they don't care about the quality of work they've done."

"No offense, Mr. Lowry, but I didn't ask for your opinion." It made sense that one contractor would bash another in hopes of getting a job, especially if work was as rare as Mr. Woodland claimed it to be this time of year. Still, this was going too far. "Now if you'll excuse me, I have things to do."

"Okay. Whatever." Mr. Lowry hung up.

Unfortunately, as Sammy tucked her phone back in her pocket, she realized that Mr. Lowry hadn't been the only one yelling. Mr. Woodland and his late employee were having their own argument. It was on the other side of the room, and they were trying to be quiet, but their voices carried easily through the empty space. The way they leaned their bodies toward each other and curled their fists at their sides didn't help disguise their feelings, either.

"I can't believe you've done this to me again, Garrett! I should fire you on the spot!" A vein popped out on Mr. Woodland's neck as his skin slowly flushed red.

The crewman was much calmer about the issue, his voice quietly threatening. "For what? Being a couple minutes late? You know my car isn't reliable, and I'm lucky I got here at all."

"Sure. Like you don't have any other excuses."

Now Garrett's face grew darker. "Why do you have to keep bringing that up?"

"Because I know you. I know the truth, and you can't just keep blaming all your problems on car trouble. Now get to work." Mr. Woodland pointed a quick finger to the other side of the room, where some of the men were beginning to carefully peel back the trim so they could get to the old paneling.

"Yessir."

Sammy took her phone out again and pretended to send a text, not wanting her new contractor to know she'd been standing there watching the entire exchange. Maybe Mr. Woodland wasn't as great of a guy as she'd originally thought. It bothered her, because in an ideal world she would only support businesses and people who shared her values. But this wasn't an ideal world, and she had a contract with this man. The fact that he was a bit of a jerk to his employees didn't mean he wouldn't do a good job.

She cleared her throat a few minutes later when she walked up to him. "Okay, I think I'm going to take off. You've got my number, though, so give me a call if you need anything."

Harold smiled, the angry part of him completely invisible now. "Will do! And I'll be sure to lock up when I'm done."

Sammy left, trying to feel good about her decision. She pulled up the collar of her jacket against the rain as she trotted to her car, reminding herself that she had bigger problems to worry about than the personal issues of her contractor. She also had a full day of baking at Just Like Grandma's.

4

A DASH OF SURPRISE

A few weeks later, Sammy stood in the center of the big room at the Stargazer. The space had been almost completely transformed. It had been a dark and gloomy space before, speaking of the ghosts of the past no matter how nice it was outside.

That wasn't the case at all now. The room had formerly been walled completely in, with no windows. Sonya wasn't sure what it had been used for before her father had turned it into an illegal gambling hall, but the solid walls had served that purpose well. Now, several large windows had been installed on the long side of the room. They only looked out into the parking lot, but it was a good start that really made the space seem more inhabitable. Paired with freshly-painted drywall in a light blue and white vinyl floor, the room was much more open and inviting than Sammy imagined it had ever been. The wall sconces, gold behemoths that leaked only the slightest bit of yellow light into the room, had been replaced with overhead LED bulbs that lit up the work space.

"Wow," Sammy breathed as she walked in the door, noting that it, too, had been replaced. The old hunk of rusty metal that had kept the elements out was now a professional door with glass and a brand-new handle. "This is just amazing."

Mr. Woodland saw her as she walked in. He turned off the saw he'd been using and dusted his hand on the side of his pants. "Sammy! It's good to see you today!"

"You didn't think I could keep myself away when you're so close to being done, did you?" She could barely even look at him because she was so busy checking out the transformation. "It's like it's a completely different room!"

"That's the goal," Harold said proudly. "We just have a few small things left to do, and then it'll be complete. Oh, and your work tables arrived today. I told the delivery guy to go ahead and bring them in.

We'd be happy to get them put together and set up for you. No charge."

"Are you sure?"

"Absolutely. I have to say, you've been one of the best people we've worked for in a while. You haven't been in here breathing down our necks, and I think the guys really appreciate all the treats you bring in. It's the least we can do."

Sammy pressed her hand to her mouth, so in awe over the way the room looked. If Mr. Herzog came wandering in, it might even change his mind as to whether or not they needed a new space. While it seemed that everyone had their misgivings about Mr. Woodland when she'd first hired him, the contractor had definitely proven himself to her. "Thank you. Thank you so much, for everything you've done."

"Oh, here." Harold reached into his pocket and retrieved a set of keys. He took one key off the ring and held onto it. "These are for the new lock on the door. If you don't mind, I'll go ahead and keep one for a little longer. I'd like to get the rest of this mess cleaned up, especially since you said you wanted to have the opening on Monday."

She hadn't been sure at one point that they would

make that deadline, but Mr. Woodland had really come through. "You don't have to clean up anything. I don't mind sweeping up."

But the contractor held out his hand and shook his head. "No, no. We're the ones that made the mess, and it's my policy to leave it clean. Garrett!" He called over his shoulder to a crewman.

"Yes, sir?"

"I want every speck of dust off this floor before you leave tonight. Get the guys to help you with the tables, and make sure they're wiped down as well. Everything better be spotless, and if you leave before it is then I'll know."

Garrett grumbled something under his breath.

"What was that?" Harold snapped.

"Yes, sir."

Sammy knew she shouldn't feel guilty, but she did. "Really, I can clean it up. You've already done so much work."

"And you're paying us for that work," Mr. Woodland reminded her. "I've heard of contractors who leave sawdust all over the floor, and that's just not the way things should be. There are only a couple pieces of trim left, and I have to wait for the stain to dry on them before I can put them up. I'll come by first thing on Monday morning to put them up, if that's all right."

"Not a problem at all! Will there be any issue if I start bringing in some of our supplies over the weekend?" Sammy knew she had a lot of work ahead of her if she was going to get this place opened on time. Rob would help with some of it, but she wanted to be as involved as possible. That would include not only getting their office area set up, but also planning for a big party on Monday night.

"I don't see why it would be. All the paint is dry and the lighting is wired up. I can't wait to see how it looks when you're done!" He smiled at her.

Sammy grinned, as excited as a little kid on Christmas morning. "Great! Thank you again for everything you've done. This is better than I ever could've imagined."

As she anticipated, the weekend was a busy one. There was plenty of work to be done at the diner, even though Helen tried to tell her to take the time off. "Go and get your new place set up. You've worked hard for this, and you deserve the time to enjoy it."

"And leave you high and dry without a waitress on a weekend? That doesn't seem fair." Sammy wiped down a table and set down new silverware. "Just Like Grandma's is my first obligation."

"But it's certainly not the biggest one. If you want some time, then take it. If you don't, well don't blame me." Helen smiled as she stepped behind the counter to take a payment.

In between customers and orders for the diner, Sammy baked her heart out. She invited Austin to come by after hours to help, and they churned out enough cookies to make a massive tray to bring to the opening party. "You're going to love this, Austin. Sunny Cove Services will be a way for you to almost always have work, whenever you want it. And there will be different kinds of work to do, too, so you won't get bored."

He carefully rolled balls of cookie dough and set them on a baking sheet. "I won't get to work with you?"

"You will," she assured him, "but just not all the time. There will be other people to help, too. That way you can still work even if I'm not available."

He stopped his work, letting his dough-covered hands drop to his sides. "But I like working with you."

Her heart broke at those words. "Oh, Austin. I like working with you, too. And I still will, every time I get the chance. But you know how there hasn't been much snow to shovel over the winter?"

Austin nodded, still wearing a sad look on his face.

"Well, you won't have to wait around for snow, and we won't have to go from house to house or around to businesses to find jobs. People will come to *you* when they need something done, and there will be things you can do indoors, too." While most of the grant money had been used up with the renovations and the rent deposit, Rob had donated an industrial paper shredder.

"Really?" Some of the spark was coming back to Austin's bright green eyes.

"Yeah. And it won't just be you working, either. There are other people out there just like you who need jobs. It'll be a great chance for you to make new friends."

His eyes roved around in his head as he processed this. "That sounds like fun!"

"I think it will be. And we're going to have a big party to celebrate. Do you need me to come pick you up on Monday night, or is Uncle Mitch going to bring you?"

Austin placed the last ball of dough on the sheet. "He said he would bring me. Uncle Mitch wants to see it."

"Wonderful." The older man had been a bit skeptical when Sammy had first begun helping Austin find employment, but he was beginning to see how much it benefitted his nephew.

When they were finished with the cookies, Sammy dropped Austin off at his place and ran over to the Stargazer. It was a Sunday afternoon, but they only had so much time to get things done before they opened. Rob's car was already in the parking lot, and she found him standing in the middle of the work room. Seeing the awe and joy on his face made her realize just how happy she must've looked when she first saw it.

"Wow. Just wow. I admit I had my doubts. I mean, I know I picked out the location, but I didn't realize it could go through this kind of transformation." He ran a hand through his blonde hair as he turned in a slow circle.

"Isn't it amazing? And to think, everyone was so concerned about the contractor I hired. Even Andrew Herzog came over here to tell me I shouldn't use him."

Rob flapped one hand in the air. "That's just because Mr. Woodland won't work with Andrew. He doesn't like his designs, and he'd rather do simple, classy stuff than all those sleek, modern schemes. I think there might be more to the equation, but I'm not sure. At any rate, this looks fantastic."

Sonya McTavish walked in from the door that led into the theater. "I agree," she purred, smiling. "My father would have an absolute fit if he could see how modern this looks compared to that crumbling old room. I love it!"

Rob took off his overcoat and laid it on a nearby chair. "I've already brought in the filing cabinets. Shall we got get things arranged in the office?"

"Ready whenever you are!" Sammy should have been tired from the work she'd already done baking, but her excitement overwhelmed all that. She'd even gotten up early to make sure she got to church on time, and she knew she wouldn't go to bed until it was late, but in the end she knew it was all worth it. She and Rob spent a lot of time arranging, talking, and planning, and when they were finally ready to shut the lights off at the end of the night she took a big sigh of happiness.

"What about those pieces of trim over there by the bathroom door?" Rob asked as they took one last survey of the room.

"Mr. Woodland said he was waiting for the stain to dry, but he'll come in first thing tomorrow morning and get them put up. Everything should be fine."

Rob looked at her, the pride clear on his face. "Are we ready to do this?"

"Definitely."

Sammy could hardly sleep that night. When she did doze off, she only dreamed of the new business and what she hoped would happen there. She envisioned all the people who would be gainfully employed, and the self-worth they would come to feel as a result. It was so thrilling she could barely take it, and every time she woke up she had a smile on her face.

When her alarm finally went off, Sammy jumped up out of bed and got dressed as quickly as possible before running down the stairs to the diner. Helen wasn't in yet, and she didn't have to be at Sunny Cove Services yet, but Sammy couldn't wait any longer. She loaded the boxes of baked goods in the back of her SUV and ran back into the diner for jugs of tea and milk as well as a coffee carafe. The party wasn't until the evening, when her friends and anyone associated with helping to get this business off the ground could get off work to attend, but Sammy wanted to make sure everything was perfect.

Driving through town, she wished she'd thought to pick up some balloons and crepe paper to really make the place look festive. SCS—as she was starting to think of it—looked great, but there was nothing wrong with giving it that special touch for the opening. Maybe she could run to the party supply store once it opened and get that taken care of.

Harold's van was parked outside the door, Woodland Contracting written in vinyl lettering across the white paint. Sammy had gotten used to seeing it there, and a renewed rush of gratitude spread through her for all that the contractor had done. He'd been a little hard on his workers, and there were a few days when he'd seemed too busy to talk to her, but in the end he'd done an excellent job. She couldn't argue with the price, either, considering some of the other contractors had asked for more money than they'd gotten with the grant. Sammy decided she would write him a personal thank you note so he knew just how much she appreciated him.

Parking next to the van, Sammy retrieved the boxes from the back of her car. She would be a little embarrassed when Harold saw how early she'd arrived, but at least the door would be unlocked. That would make it a lot easier to get all these packages inside.

But when Sammy pushed her shoulder against the door, it didn't budge. She paused, staring at the door for a moment. Glancing through the glass, she could see that the lights were on in the building. Maybe Harold had gone in, but he'd locked the door behind him for safety's sake. It was a small town, the kind of place where people rarely even locked their doors and windows at night, but she could see why he would want to be extra careful. He probably had a lot of expensive tools to protect.

Juggling the boxes in her right hand she carefully fished out the key with her left hand. Sammy nearly dropped the boxes as they tipped over in her grasp, threatening to go spilling across the wet asphalt and letting all of her hard work go to waste. Sammy dove to the side to catch them, bracing them against the doorway as she unlocked the building.

"That was close," Sammy whispered to herself as she shakily put the key in the lock. She pushed her way into the building with both hands on the boxes now so that she wouldn't drop them before she made it to the big table at the back of the room where they were going to set up all of the party food. The space seemed awfully quiet without even the radio that the crewmen usually listened to while they worked. Sammy shrugged, figuring that Harold probably preferred peace and quiet first thing in the morning and began setting up.

She arranged the boxes of cookies on the table. Next to the chocolate chip and iced sugar cookies, she placed the snickerdoodles that she and Austin had so carefully made. He had truly enjoyed rolling the little balls of dough in the cinnamon and sugar, and Sammy knew that the other folks she would be helping out at Sunny Cove Services would probably feel the same way once they got a chance to have their baking lessons with her as well. Next, she laid out oatmeal raisin cookies, red velvet cookies that she normally only made at Christmas time, and a large assortment of sprinkled cookies that Austin had personally decorated. It looked good even with the treats still in the boxes, and it would look even better when she laid them out for the party.

The coffee carafe went on the table next to the cookies, although she wouldn't be able to make the coffee until closer to time for the party. Sammy arranged stacks of plates, cups, and napkins before stepping into the small break area to put the jugs of milk and tea in the fridge.

It was as she came back into the main part of the room that she realized she hadn't seen Harold at all. He should be here, especially considering that those little pieces of trim had yet to be put up. "Harold? Are you here?" She knocked on the bathroom door, and when she got no answer she dared to open it. The lights came on automatically when they detected movement—something that seemed like a good idea to save energy even though the sensors cost a little extra money—but they only revealed a clean, newly remodeled bathroom.

"Huh." She chewed the inside of her cheek. If he'd forgotten something and had to run back to his place for a tool, then his van wouldn't still be here. Realizing he might still be in his van, Sammy trotted to the door and peeked outside. She could see right into the windshield of the big vehicle, but there was still no sign of the contractor.

Walking back through the main part of the room between the work tables, Sammy pulled her phone out of her pocket and dialed Harold's number. She waited patiently as it started to ring, but she soon realized that she wasn't just hearing the ring in the receiver. The tiny beeping tune was coming from the room she was in. Harold was here somewhere.

Following the sound, she wound her way through the tables to a desk intended for a supervisor they had yet to hire. A work boot stuck out from the side of it, slackly tipped to the side.

"Harold!" Sammy dove around the desk, her blood icing over as she saw him. His face was pale, his eyes staring at the ceiling. She started to ask him if he was all right, but the answer was clear to her right away. Blood soaked the front of his shirt, staining the worn blue into a deep purple. A battery-operated nail gun lay at his side.

Fighting the urge to throw up, Sammy dashed outside to call the police.

5

HALF A STICK OF SUSPICION

"Honey, really. If there was ever a time when you needed to be off work, I'd think it would be now. Go upstairs, make yourself a nice hot cup of tea, and rest."

"I can't," Sammy choked out. Her face felt hot and tired from crying, but she continued mixing up the dough for a batch of dinner rolls. "The very last thing I want is to be upstairs alone. I need work to keep me sane right now." She'd already prayed her heart out, and that had gone a long way toward making her feel better, but she wanted to be busy. There was always plenty of work to be done at Just Like Grandma's, and it made her feel like she was making up for some of the time she'd missed while trying to start of SCS.

"I understand. I'm just worried about you, dear. I know how you were looking forward to this day."

"It's not just me. It's Austin, too, and everyone else. Even Rob seemed upset. I never thought a former jock like him would be so into something for the community. And it's rather disturbing what happened to Mr. Woodland, too."

Helen laid a comforting hand on her back. "I know, dear. But Alfie is doing everything he can, I'm sure."

It usually amused Sammy when the older woman referred to the sheriff by his childhood nickname from when he'd grown up across the street from her, but she failed to see the humor in the moment. "Yes, I'm sure he is. He didn't let me stick around very long. He even had one of the officers put all those cookies back in my car for me. That was nice, but I'm not sure what to do with them now. There's obviously no party, but I don't really feel right selling them."

"Maybe we can find someplace to donate them," Helen offered with a smile. "Or we can just sit back here and stuff our faces after the customers go home."

Sammy had to laugh a little at that. "I just might do that! It's a tragedy, and I feel so selfish."

"Why's that?"

She looked up from the mixing bowl to meet her boss's eyes. "I know the important thing here is that Mr. Woodland is dead. There's nothing bigger than that. But all I can think about is that nobody is going to be interested in supporting Sunny Cove Services if they think of it as the site of a murder. I really need the community's help with this. Not financially, necessarily, but I need their willingness to hire these people and keep them employed. And I'm a little worried that nobody will want to work there after something like this has happened."

Helen put one hand on her ample hip. "Don't you think someone has probably died in most of the buildings around here?"

"What do you mean?"

"Well, think about it. There are a lot of very old buildings in Sunny Cove. Just the amount of time they've been standing makes it seem to me pretty likely that *something* has happened in most of them. I'm sure you could go to the library, look through old editions of the newspaper, and find a tragic event of some sort in nearly every building in this town. It doesn't mean that it's cursed or that people won't go there. They'll just need a little time to get past it."

Sammy smiled for the first time since she'd discovered Harold's body, and it felt good. "Have you always been able to look at the positive side of things, Helen?"

"I always try," she replied kindly. "I've got Jesus at my side to help me remember, but I thoroughly believe that a positive attitude can make all the difference in the world."

"Yeah, you're right."

When they'd closed the diner for the night and Sammy had finally dragged herself upstairs to her apartment, she took a moment to close her eyes and remember everything she had to be grateful for. Even though the contractor's death had tainted her excitement over the opening of SCS, she still had a great business partner who'd done so much to help this project along. She had Helen, and she had Austin. It didn't hurt that she still had her job at the diner, so it wasn't as though she'd been counting on the new business to be a source of income for her. With a little help from Heaven, this could still turn out all right.

And Sammy also knew that the Lord helps those

who trust in Him. The police were doing their job, as Helen had said, but that didn't mean she couldn't help. Turning to a clean page in her notebook, she tapped her pen against her chin as she began making a list of suspects.

First, there was Ken Lowry. The contractor was in direct competition with Harold Woodland, and he'd been very angry when he'd discovered he hadn't gotten the job. Could he have been mad enough to kill?

Underneath his name she wrote that of Andrew Herzog. Sammy had thought the land developer was guilty of murder before, when he'd been advocating for tearing down a historical building to construct a new condo. The Radical Grandmas had been strictly against him, and when one of them turned up dead Mr. Herzog was one of the first people Sammy thought of. He had a bit of a cutthroat attitude when it came to progress. While he'd proven to be innocent at that time, he'd definitely thought using the Stargazer Theater was a mistake. Would have made him upset enough to murder someone? Probably not, but Sammy wasn't going to look past anyone.

Thinking of Andrew brought to mind Jackson and Sons, the contracting company from Oak Hills that

Andrew had recommended. As far as Sammy knew, they didn't know much about Harold Woodland. They would have no real reason to kill him, considering that remodeling the old space was probably not the kind of thing they normally did. But once again, she didn't want to dismiss anyone too soon. It would at least be a lead to chase down, even if only so she could cross them off the list.

Stumped, Sammy got up and put the kettle on. Helen's suggestion of a cup of hot tea hadn't been a bad one, and she had a big box of chamomile just waiting for a night like tonight. The rain drizzled down the windows and tap danced on the roof just above her head. Sammy couldn't see anything through the darkness outside her kitchen window other than the streetlights, each with a humid halo around them. "Who else would want to kill Mr. Woodland?" she mused quietly to herself. Her voice sounded too loud in the quiet space.

A mug of tea in hand, Sammy returned to the kitchen table. This had become her thinking space, an area where she made lists and plans. Sometimes those lists and plans had involved finding a murderer, but they'd also revolved around experimenting with new recipes or coming up with ideas to further her baked goods business. The old wooden chairs were surprisingly comfortable, and Sammy felt cozy and safe in her little apartment. She leaned back and tipped her chin toward the ceiling, thinking.

A thump on the door brought her upright with a jolt. Sammy had nearly dozed off, but she was wide awake now. She hadn't even heard anyone come up the stairs. "Who is it?"

"Sheriff Jones," came the muffled reply through the door.

"Oh." Sammy quickly opened it, suddenly self-conscious about the sweatpants and hoodie she'd thrown on after work. "What are you doing here? I mean, what can I do for you?"

He gave her a slight smile, something that wasn't often seen on his solemn face. Alfred Jones was a tall, muscular man with natural tan that complimented his dark hair. There were streaks of silver through it, but he still looked young for his age. He took off his hat and strode into the apartment, still in uniform. "Mostly, I wanted to make sure you were all right. You were pretty upset at the theater today."

Sammy didn't know if she should be flattered that he cared or insulted to think she couldn't handle it. "I've been better," she admitted. "But how did you get in here? Did I not lock the outside door?" The stairs that led down from her apartment door opened up into the back room of the diner, so anyone who wanted to get in had to get into Just Like Grandma's first.

"You did," he reassured her, "but I ran into Helen down at the store. I told her I was concerned, and she came over here and let me in. I told her I'd lock it back up when I left."

"I see." Sammy pressed her lips together and rocked back on her heels, wondering just what Helen was up to. Her boss had dropped some hints from time to time that she and Sheriff Jones would make a good couple, and she had to wonder if Helen was pushing this further along.

He nodded toward the notebook on the table, just a few feet away. "Dare I ask what you're doing?"

There was no point in trying to hide it. He'd seen her lists before, and this wasn't the first time she'd tried to find a killer. "You can ask, but you probably won't want to hear the answer."

Raising one eyebrow, he turned the notebook so he could see. He read it quickly, giving a slight nod. "Not a bad start."

"And?"

"And I think you need to leave this to the police, Sammy. There's a lot to deal with on a case like this, and you really don't need to get involved."

Her heart jumped up in her throat. "Is there someone dangerous out there?"

Sheriff Jones tipped his head to the side. "I don't know if I'd say that. I shouldn't say anything, really, but I think if I tell you it might ease your mind a little."

"What is it?" She could barely get the words out around the tightness in her throat.

He sighed. "There was a note in Harold Woodland's pocket. It looked like the start of a suicide note, so there's a good possibility he killed himself."

Sammy sank slowly into one of the kitchen chairs. "I'm not sure that makes me feel better at all." She didn't like thinking about what might happen to his soul. She also didn't like to think that someone she'd come to know over the past few weeks was feeling hopeless enough to do such a thing and she hadn't noticed.

"Well, we don't have all the details yet. We're working on it, though, and we don't draw any conclusions until we're absolutely sure. I just want you to know."

"I do know." She propped her chin on her hand, feeling depressed all over again. "I just wish I could go back and change it all. Maybe if I hadn't hired him, this wouldn't have happened."

"Whoa, hey now." Jones sat down across from her, tipping his head down to catch her eyes. "Don't talk like this is your fault. We could blame ourselves for every bad thing that happens around us, or we can move on and understand that we don't have control over it all."

She reached out a finger and poked at the notebook. "I guess I like having a little bit of control. Maybe that's why I like to do this."

"I can understand that." Jones looked at the list again. "Maybe we can figure out if there's anyone else who belongs on this list."

That got Sammy smiling. He was probably just humoring her, but it was a sweet gesture. "I'm being rude. Can I get you a cup of tea?"

"Sure."

She got up and went back to the stove. The kettle was still hot, and she poured a second mug of tea. "I have a bunch of leftover cookies here, too, if you'd like some. More than I know what to do with, unfortunately."

"I don't think I can pass up a chance at Sammy Baker's famous cookies, especially not if I'm getting them for free."

Sammy blushed as she handed him a plate with an assortment of cookies. "Okay, now tell me who else you think belongs on this list."

"No, no. You're supposed to tell me. You're the detective genius who's supposed to give me all my ideas so I can take credit for them."

Sammy laughed. "All right, then. How about Julia Richardson. She saw that I was interviewing Woodland, and she told me I shouldn't use him because he did a shoddy job on her bathroom. I wouldn't think that it would be enough motive to kill someone, but I didn't see how bad of a job he did. Maybe it brought up some old memories."

He nodded and slid the notebook toward her. "Probably worth putting her on the list. I mean, in case it wasn't a suicide. Anyone else?"

"I haven't been able to come up with anyone," she admitted. "I'll be sure to let you know when I do."

The two of them ate the plate of cookies and drank the rest of their tea as they discussed the other options on the list and tossed around a few other ideas. In the end, they didn't write down any more names, but Sammy felt a little bit better.

"I appreciate you stopping by," she said when Jones got up to go. "I'm still worried about how SCS is going to do, because I've put so much work into it, but maybe it'll be okay."

A strange look crossed his face and left just as quickly as it had come. "Yeah, so, you and Rob Hewitt, huh?"

"Hmm?"

"The two of you have been spending a lot of time together, lately."

She could feel her face coloring, but mostly just because he asked the question. "Oh, no. It's not like that. We've just been putting in a lot of time on this project."

"I see. I'd heard some rumors."

"Just friends," she said, feeling like she was back in high school all over again.

"You have a good night, and I'll be sure the door is locked downstairs."

"Thanks." Sammy shut the door gently behind him, feeling a little too giddy.

When she went to bed a little later, her mind turned back to the list as she realized there was someone she'd forgotten. Harold hadn't been very easy on his workers, especially that man with the dark hair. She quickly added Garrett's name with a question mark after it, since she didn't know his surname, and went to bed.

6
TWO HEAPING TABLESPOONS OF TOWN GOSSIP

The diner wasn't very busy the next day, but Sammy wished it was. She liked the distraction. Quite a few people popped in to pick up pastries or doughnuts, but most of them didn't stay to eat.

Except for Julia Richardson, who lingered at her favorite table while she slowly ate the soup of the day—a delicious lentil soup that Helen had put together—and then leisurely drank a few cups of coffee. Sammy was spending most of her time in the kitchen, but she happened to be the one to come out and pick up her check.

"Oh, Sammy! I didn't think you were here. I wanted to talk to you about something."

She couldn't make any excuses about being busy,

considering the restaurant was nearly deserted. And the truth was that she wanted to get started on her list. "What can I do for you?"

"It's more of what I can do for you," Mrs. Richardson explained. "I wanted to say I'm sorry about what happened to your contractor. To be fair, I warned you not to use him, but I can't say I expected *that* to happen. And now you have to wait to open."

"It'll be all right," Sammy assured her with a forced smile. "We'll get it all figured out."

"Sit down, dear, sit down." Mrs. Richardson gestured at the seat across from her. "I've heard about how you've been involved in a few of the strange things that happen around this town. I thought I might have some information that would help you out."

Sammy sat, but she shook her head and waved off the customer's notions. "This is a police matter, and it doesn't have anything to do with me."

"Pish tosh! You can't kid a kidder, sweetheart! I know you're at least thinking about it."

She could at least humor her, and in the process she might learn something. "Okay. Lay it on me."

Mrs. Richardson leaned forward. "Harold Woodland had been working in Sunny Cove for a very long time. He was known as a shrewd businessman, and it worked well for him for a long time. But the more money he made, the greedier he became."

It sounded like quite the parable, but Sammy was interested in what she had to say. "I'm listening."

"While I can't talk poorly of him for wanting to make money, it was his methods that really made people start talking about him. He started using cheap materials that didn't hold up, he cut corners to the detriment of his customers, and he wasn't very nice to the men who worked for him. Why, there was one young man helping him with that bathroom of mine, and Mr. Woodland did nothing but yell at him the entire time!"

The contractor had seemed very nice when Sammy had interviewed him, but she was starting to understand that she hadn't seen the entire picture. "I can't say anything yet about the work he did or the quality of it. Things seems fine at SCS so far, but only time will tell. As for the workers, well, I did see some of that myself."

"And then there's his poor wife!" Julia exclaimed.

"His wife?" Somehow, Sammy hadn't thought about Mr. Woodland in terms of his family at all yet.

"Oh, yes. High school sweethearts, those two. But he was never home because he was working all the time, staying out late at night or working on the weekends to get his projects done. It really upset poor Tracy. She tried to drag him to counseling a few times, dear thing, but it didn't do them much good."

Sammy licked her lips, thinking. "How do you know all this about them?"

Julia flicked her bedazzled fingers in the air. "Simple. He's my cousin."

"What?" Sammy stared across the table at Mrs. Richardson for a long moment. "He's your cousin? And you still didn't think I should hire him?"

"Blood is blood, and I would do whatever I could for family, but not if they're going to rip people off or break their promises. Harold was a bit of a black sheep, I guess you could say."

"I see." It was all very interesting. While the fact that Julia was related to Harold would seem to keep her off the list of suspects, Sammy wasn't ready to cross her off just yet. She could've told Sammy all these stories to get her to look to someone else as the murderer. The truth was that she seemed like more of town gossip than a killer, but Sammy was learning not to assume anything about anyone. "I appreciate you spending a little time talking to me."

"Anytime, dear. If you have questions or you need me to go on a covert mission, you just let me know. I don't have a whole lot filling up my social calendar these days, and I could use a little excitement." She winked as she handed Sammy her check and her payment.

That evening, once she'd finished closing up the restaurant and was headed upstairs to make a few notes on her list and add Tracy Woodland to it, Sammy's phone rang. She recognized the number, but it wasn't one she'd saved in her phone. "Hello?"

"Samantha, this is Ken Lowry. How are you?"

"Fine, thank you." It was one of the other contractors, one she hadn't hired and who'd been rather upset when he found out about it. Sammy paused on the steps. "What can I do for you?"

"It's more a matter of what I can do for you. I heard about what happened to Harold, and I thought you might need someone to come finish up the work at the theater. I'm available, if you need me."

Sammy slowly started walking up the steps again, thinking. The couple of pieces of trim that had yet to be put up weren't too much work. She could do it, or she could find someone willing to spend a few minutes on it. Maybe even Rob knew how to do that sort of thing, though she doubted it. Still, Lowry was on her list of suspects, and this could provide the perfect opportunity for her to talk to him. "There's not much, but a little help would be great. I can meet you at the Stargazer at eight tomorrow morning."

"I'll be there!" He sounded happy as he rang off, but Sammy had to wonder if this was a mistake. If the contractor was a killer, then she was putting herself in danger. Jones had explained that Woodland's death was a potential suicide, and he'd told her to stay out of it, but she hadn't exactly made it a habit to follow his directions.

7

AN OUNCE OF RIVALRY

S unny Cove Services looked much the same as it had when Sammy had come in Monday morning planning to have an opening party, but it certainly had a different feel to it. The excitement she'd experienced was replaced by apprehension and even a little fear. Sammy turned on the lights, wishing she'd thought to bring someone with her. On the other hand, if Ken Lowry turned out to be dangerous, then she would only be risking the safety of anyone she asked to come. And she certainly couldn't have brought Sheriff Jones, considering he didn't want her to be involved at all.

Lowry showed up only a couple of minutes later, carrying an old-fashioned wooden toolbox in one hand. He strode into the room and held out his hand to shake Sammy's. He looked to be about the same age as Harold had been, perhaps in his late forties, but he'd retained much more of his hair. "It's good to see you again. Tell me what still needs to be done."

"Honestly, there isn't much. There are just a few pieces of trim that need to go in here by the bathroom. I don't think there was a whole lot else."

The contractor frowned as she examined the doorway she pointed to. "I see. Yeah, that wouldn't take much. Looks like the drywall wasn't done very well around the light switches and outlets. I also would've gone with a higher quality flooring. That can't be changed now, not reasonably, but you'll end up needing to get new flooring within just a few years. Only a little more money would've gotten you something with a lifetime warranty."

"I'll keep that in mind." Sammy frowned at the floor, wishing she'd known to ask such questions of Harold.

Ken plucked a small level out of his toolbox and set it on a windowsill, bending down to see where the bubble landed. "Not too bad, but it could've been better."

Remembering what Mrs. Richardson had said, Sammy cleared her throat. "Has it been your experience that Mr. Woodland usually did inferior work?"

The contractor ran a hand through his shaggy dark hair. "Harold and I had quite the rivalry, but it was always in a good-natured way. This town isn't really big enough for the number of contractors we have here, but that never stopped any of us from trying to live our dreams. You know, he and I even had wood shop together back in high school. We were always competing to see who could build the best stool or birdhouse."

"I got the impression there was a bit more animosity between the two of you. You seemed quite upset when I hired him." Sammy held her breath, wondering what he would say.

"I'm sorry about that," came his genuine reply. Lowry's drooping brown eyes looked into hers pleadingly. "I hope you'll forgive me for being so unprofessional. It's been a tough year, and I haven't gotten nearly enough work to keep all my creditors at bay. I overreacted."

Sammy smiled, starting to feel that her life wasn't in danger with this man around. "It's all right. I understand. We all have our days."

He pointed at the bathroom doorway. "I can have

that trim put up for you in no time. There are a few things I would've done differently with the remodel, but I don't think any of it is a big enough deal to worry about. Do you have anything else you need me to do?"

Mr. Lowry was really trying to be kind to her, and Sammy wished she did have more work for him, but the truth was that Woodland had fairly well taken care of all of it. "Honestly, no. But I'll be sure to keep your card in case we need anything in the future."

"Thanks. I'll get this taken care of right now." He picked up the pieces of trim where they were propped up near the wall and set them in place to see how they fit.

Sammy's phone rang. "Excuse me a moment." She stepped into the office to answer.

"Ms. Baker, this is Beau Jackson from Jackson and Sons Contracting in Oak Grove. I understand you might be needing our services."

She rolled her eyes toward the ceiling, praying for patience. "I can't say that I do, I'm sorry."

"Are you sure? I heard about what happened to Woodland, and I know he was working for you.

That must've cut the job short, and he had quite the reputation for not finishing his jobs."

Sammy could see Ken from where she stood, finishing up the trim. "Everything is taken care of, but thank you."

The man on the other end of the line sighed. "If you're sure. But I'm more than happy to come take a look at the place. There might be some things that still need to be done that you aren't aware of."

"With all due respect, I've got it figured out. But thanks again." She made a few polite excuses and hung up, feeling irritated.

"All done," Lowry announced as she came out of the office.

"What do I owe you?"

He shook his head. "Not a thing. This didn't take much time, and I'm sure I owed Harold a favor anyway. I wish you the best of luck with this place. It'll be a good thing for our town."

As he walked out the door, Rob Hewitt walked in. "Hey, Sammy. I saw your car and that guy's van out front. What's going on?"

She briefly explained the situation, but only the part

about getting the trim finished. He didn't need to know about her list of suspected killers. "And I just had a call from Jackson and Sons. I feel like I should be happy that we have people willing to step in, but I can't help but feel like they're just trying to take advantage of the situation."

Rob nodded. "I'm sure, at least in some way, they are. Everyone knows about the grant we got, and it probably sounds like a lot of money to anyone who hasn't tried to start up a business. They want to get a piece of the pie, so to speak, and things are a little tight for everyone around here lately. I should know, considering quite a few of my clients are behind on making their payments."

This caught her off-guard. "You let them make payments to you?" Rob was a very prominent attorney, and he handled all the biggest cases. Sammy hadn't imagined that he would run his business like that.

"Of course. If I didn't, they'd never be able to pay me at all. That wouldn't be very good business, especially not in a place like Sunny Cove."

Sammy smiled. She'd definitely misjudged Rob when she'd first come back to town. He was a much kinder, more generous man than she'd thought. Still, the sheriff's suspicions about the two of them were way off. She liked him as a friend, but she knew they were completely different people. "Do you think we'll ever get to open?"

"Oh yeah. Just give it a little time. Let Jones and his boys get this whole thing cleared up, and then we can get back on track. I don't mean to sound cold about it, but we also can't let this get in the way of what we want to do here. There are a lot of people counting on us."

Sammy thought of Austin and how disappointed he'd been when he'd found out they couldn't have the opening party and that he couldn't get started on his new job right away. She'd sent him home with two big boxes of the cookies he'd helped to make, but that wasn't the same for him. "You're right. There are. I just wish there was something we could do right now to help things along."

Rob bobbed his head in agreement. "I do, too, but I think we just have to stand back and wait for the moment."

8

A PINT OF PATIENCE

The weather was rainy and miserable again the next day, and it affected business at Just Like Grandma's. A few people came in to get a bowl of soup or a cup of coffee to warm up, but those who did stop in didn't stay long or get very chatty. They pulled on their raincoats and trudged back out the door, ducking into doorways and diving into their cars to get away from the wetness. Small rivers had formed in the gutters, and the only people who seemed to enjoy the weather were small children in rubber boots.

Sammy had been eager for a distraction the first few days after Harold's death, but today she was glad for the relief. She was completely exhausted. She'd been emotionally wrung out from trying to open Sunny Cove Services and finding the contractor's body, and it hadn't helped that she'd been staying up far too late at night while she thought about her list. She'd crossed off Ken Lowry and Julia Richardson, but she knew there was still work to do. Several times, Sammy had considered calling Sheriff Jones to ask him if they'd discovered any more about the note, but she'd stopped herself. He would let her know if they found anything important. Wouldn't he?

The lunch rush wasn't much of a rush at all, but it brought in a man who looked vaguely familiar to Sammy. He had dark hair and a muscular build, and he sat alone at the counter to scarf down a burger and fries.

"You look down," she said as she refilled his iced tea. Helen often made conversation with the customers, and Sammy had come to realize this was not only good business but quite fun. She like chatting with both strangers and the locals she'd come to know. "If Johnny botched your burger, I'd be happy to have him make a new one."

"No, no. It's fine. I'm just out of work right now." He picked up a French fry and lazily poked his ketchup with it.

"I've heard that a lot around town lately. Oh, wait. You worked for Harold Woodland, didn't you?" The words came out before she had a chance to think about them, since that might not have been the smartest thing to say. "Garrett, right?"

He lifted his eyebrows for a moment, as if to say his identity wasn't anything to get excited about. "That's me."

"I'm very sorry about what happened to your boss. Can't you get work with one of the other contractors in town?"

Garrett sighed. "Not too likely. I don't think they have any work for me, and they wouldn't want me anyway."

"That's not a very positive attitude to have about it. Why wouldn't they want you?" Sammy always felt the need to help others, even if it was just discussing their problems with them. It shouldn't affect her at all if this guy didn't have a job, but she didn't like to think that anyone might be sad.

"It's a long story, and I won't go into it."

"I would think your time with Mr. Woodland would mean something."

He glared at her for a moment before looking down at his plate again. "Not likely."

"So what are you going to do?" she pressed.

"I'll tell you what I'm going to do. I'm going to get out of this tiny town and head to a bigger city, one with more opportunities and where people don't know me so well." He pulled a few bills and put them on the counter. "Thanks for lunch."

Sammy wanted to call him back and tell him she would help him find a place. It deeply bothered her to see someone so down in the dumps, and she wanted to do something about it. But as she watched him slink off to his car, which was parked along the street in front of the diner, she could see that he was serious about leaving town. His vehicle was packed to the gills, the windows blocked by boxes and bags. Garrett had already gathered all of his belongings, and he was ready to get out of Sunny Cove.

She sighed. He probably wasn't the first person to get tired of small-town life and decide there was something better for him elsewhere. But Garrett had been one of the suspects on her list after the way Harold had treated him.

If he was leaving town, then Sheriff Jones should probably know. But Sammy didn't have any definitive evidence that he'd done anything wrong, and she'd better have some solid proof if she was going to let him know that she was pursuing this case. Even though the sheriff had sat down and gone over his list with her, he had insisted that she leave the investigating up to him. Sammy sighed. She would have to wait.

"I don't think he's your type," Helen said over her shoulder.

"What?" Sammy turned to look at her boss.

"I don't think I've ever seen you staring at someone that hard," Helen said with a wink.

Sammy laughed. "No, nothing like that. I was just thinking."

"That doesn't have anything to do with Harold Woodland, does it? I mean, I'm sure Alfie doesn't want you sniffing around his case." She raised an eyebrow as she picked up Garrett's plate.

"He says that, but if it's true, then maybe he needs to work his cases a little harder." Sammy hadn't confronted her boss about letting the sheriff into the diner the other night, but she wasn't sure she was going to. It'd been fun to sit down with Jones and talk about the suspects, and she'd needed the company more than she'd realized.

"Maybe he should. Who's next on your list?"

Sammy followed Helen to the kitchen, wondering how much Jones had told his former neighbor. "Who says I have a list?"

The older woman laughed as she rinsed the plate. "Oh, honey. Don't you think I know you better than that? In fact, I think just about everyone knows you better than that."

"All right, then. I do have a few people I'd like to talk to about the matter."

Helen patted her shoulder. "I'd like to tell you that you should listen to Alfie and leave this matter alone, and that it's no place for a woman. Not because I really feel that way, but because I don't want you getting yourself into trouble. Still, I know I can't stop you from doing anything you've set your mind to. Just be careful, all right?"

Sammy nodded. "I will," she promised. "You want to be the Watson to my Sherlock? You know a lot of people in this town, and far better than I do."

"I think I'll pass this time. I'm tired and I'm ready to go put my feet up and catch up on my soaps. Besides, I know the case is in good hands." She headed back out to the dining floor.

"Is it?" Sammy mused to herself. She shifted her

weight on her feet, considering whether or not she should call Jones. If the note had proven to be a suicide note, then there was no point in Sammy pursuing this mystery. It would mean there really wasn't a mystery at all, and all of her efforts would just be a waste of time.

She needed to do something, and there was one thing she was very good at. Sammy got out the flour and the butter and started baking.

9

ONE QUART OF UNDERSTANDING

The rain had stopped, but the puddles that had gathered on the sidewalks had yet to dissipate. The air was cold and humid, and Sammy hunched her shoulders up around her neck as she loaded up her SUV. She thought of her grandmother as she bundled the packages into the back of the vehicle, wondering if that was where she'd gotten her knack for food. Grandma Beaumont had always been so eager to feed anyone who was at her house, even if they didn't plan to stay for very long. The scent of fresh cookies or bread constantly hung in the air, and she insisted that her guests come in to sit down.

While her grandma didn't get out of the house much in her old age, the one thing she did do was take food to those who'd been through rough times.

When the Marshalls had lost their home to a fire, Grandma B had tracked them down at a nearby hotel and brought them a large casserole and a cake. When someone she went to church with lost a family member, Grandma headed to the kitchen before doing anything else. She supplied all the grieving and downtrodden with nourishment.

Sammy had questioned this once when she was about thirteen. "A pie isn't going to bring Mr. Reynolds back from the dead," she'd sassed from the breakfast bar.

Grandma had raised one gray eyebrow, looking like she was ready to pop Sammy's cheek for such impertinence. Instead, she leaned heavily on the counter and took her granddaughter's hand. "Of course, it won't. I don't for a moment deceive myself that it will. But it might make them feel a little better to know that I'm thinking about them and praying for them. At the very least, Mrs. Reynolds won't have to worry about cooking while she's mourning her husband. You'll understand it when you're older."

Sammy hadn't been so sure at the time, but she was now. When she'd gotten off work, she knew she had to do something about Harold Woodland's death. She couldn't bring him back to life, and she might not even be able to find his killer. But she could bring cookies and condolences to his widow, something she should've done much sooner.

As she splashed through the puddles on her way to the address on Harold's business card, Sammy wondered just how rough things had been between the late contractor and his wife. Julia Richardson indicated they had plenty of troubles. She might have known that to be true, or she might've been exaggerating to make a better story. Sammy would find out soon enough.

She slowed down on Lincoln Street, looking for the right address. It was easy to find once she noticed the large sign in the front yard that read, "Harold Woodland, Contractor." The house number was only secondary information after that. It was a cute little place, painted yellow with white shutters. The window boxes and the flowerbeds that bordered the curving walkway were empty, waiting for the spring weather, but Sammy imagined it looked quite nice during the summer. A blue sedan with Tracy Woodland's initials on the license plate sat in the driveway in front of the garage, and Sammy parked behind it. "At least I know she's home."

She'd brought cookies and soup, thinking that would be appropriate for both the weather and the widow.

Instead of putting the cookies in a plain white box, Sammy had put them on a nice metal Christmas tray she'd found in the diner and covered with festive plastic wrap. The soup was in one of the typical takeout containers they used at Just Like Grandma's, which meant she had to be a bit careful with it to make sure it wouldn't spill. It was nice and warm as she carried it up to the door. Sammy should feel good about this errand, but something in the pit of her stomach was disagreeing with her. The bad feeling oozed through her bloodstream and made her hand shake as she reached up to knock.

The lights were on in the house, visible in the glass panes on either side of the door. Sammy thought she could hear the faint sound of the television, but there was no answer. She knocked a little harder, not wanting to be rude but also not wanting to stand out on the porch forever. Waiting patiently, she examined the front of the house. It looked to be quite cute from the street, but up close Sammy could see that it needed quite a bit of repair. The white paint on the door was chipped, and part of the knocker was missing. The button on the doorbell was cracked, and the shutter on the nearest window hung at an odd angle. Sammy's brow creased, wondering why a contractor wouldn't have fixed these minor details on his own house, considering he must've known how. Of course, that could've been part of the problems he and his wife had.

When there was still no answer, Sammy was about ready to give up when she noticed a sign to the left of the door. "Office" was stenciled out in faded red letters, and an arrow painted underneath it pointed to the left. While Sammy doubted anyone was in the office at this time of night, and especially now that Mr. Woodland was gone, she hadn't come all this way for nothing.

She stepped down off the porch toward the driveway, continuing on around the corner of the garage until she found a small building in the back. It had another faded sign over the door, and all the lights were on. Sammy poked her head inside.

She immediately wished she hadn't. A woman— whom she could only assume was Mrs. Woodland— was there, but she sat in a desk chair with a terrified look on her face. The muzzle of a gun was pressed against her temple. Sammy's eyes slowly followed the hand that held the gun up the adjoining arm until she saw who the owner was.

"Garrett, what are you doing?" Sammy whispered.

The pistol immediately pointed at her. "Get in here, and shut the door behind you!"

Sammy did as she was told, inwardly chiding herself for not going to Sheriff Jones right away. He might've made fun of her or even gotten angry with her, but that would've been better than having a gun pointed at her head. She slowly shut the door, still balancing the food in her free hand. "Just put the gun down, Garrett. I don't know what you think you're going to accomplish here, but this isn't the way to do it."

The worker took a step back, swiveling his pistol so he could point it easily at either of the women. "I wouldn't need to do it this way if she just would've cooperated! All I needed was a good reference on company letterhead, backdated a few days so it would look like it came from Harold. That's not so hard!"

Tracy Woodland, her mouth a thin line and her dark hair tousled, was stiff in her chair. "And I might have helped you if you hadn't been so darn rude about it!"

"Don't you dare talk to me about rude! The only thing your husband ever did was boss me around like I was some untalented grunt. And every time I tried to speak up, he just reminded me that he knew my past." Garrett's eyes were wild, and the gun shook slightly in his hand.

Sammy's lungs refused to work on their own, and she had to take a deliberate breath before speaking. "What about your past?"

His face scrunched in anger. "I guess I might as well say, because it doesn't matter now. I'm a convicted felon, and Harold hired me anyway. Acted like he was really doing me a favor, but he just wanted to use it as blackmail so he wouldn't have to pay me as much and he could get more work out of me. He said if I gave him too much lip, he'd tell the whole town and ruin what little reputation I had. I was so tired of it!"

"Is that why you killed him?" Tracy asked bitterly without turning to look at her captor. "I wasn't sure at first, but I definitely am now."

"It's not as though you really care he's gone," Garrett retorted. "I know the two of you had problems. Everyone did, and that's why I thought the police would go straight to you as soon as they discovered he was dead."

"They didn't suspect me because I didn't kill him!" Tracy snapped.

"Okay, how about everyone just calms down." Sammy noticed that several sheets of letterhead were scattered across the top of the desk, proving what Garrett had come here for. It made sense, considering that he'd already told her he was leaving for a bigger town to get a new job. As much as she would have liked to leave, she knew it wasn't the right thing to do. Leaving these two here with their tempers would only end badly. She took a hesitant step forward.

Garrett swiveled the gun to point at her. "Stop right there! I don't know why you're here, but you've got really bad timing."

"You're right." Sammy took a deep breath, her mind reeling as she tried to think of what to do. "I shouldn't be here. Do you want me to leave?"

"Do you think I'm stupid? You'll just call the cops. Give me your cell phone."

"Okay. It's in my coat pocket. I'll have to set these things down." Sammy had the container of soup in one hand and the tray of cookies in the other. She dared to look away from the gunman for a moment and down at the soup, noticing that the takeout container had once again failed to hold up to the trip. It was a long shot, but it was her best chance at getting herself out of this mess.

Sammy took another step forward, ostensibly toward the desk to set the soup down. But she lunged forward, squeezing the plastic container as hard as she could in her hand and thrusting her arm out. The hot liquid sloshed out onto Garrett, and he reeled backward to get away from it. His right hand flew up into the air, firing a shot into the ceiling. Drywall dust rained down.

Dropping the plastic container, Sammy took another step forward. Her arms and legs moved on their own now, and she wasn't even sure what she was doing as she whipped the metal cookie tray across Garrett's face. She couldn't possibly hit him hard enough to knock him out, but he was stunned.

Seeing what was happening, Tracy shot to her feet. She grabbed Garrett's arm, wrestling the gun out of his hand.

He was sprawled on the floor now, and he sneered at Mrs. Woodland. "Do you even know how to use that thing?"

She tipped the gun up and shot the face of the clock on the wall. "Yep. Seems I do." Tracy looked at Sammy. "I hope you actually have your phone with you."

"I do." She took it out of her pocket, not quite believing what had just happened even though she'd been a part of it.

"Good. Harold turned off the phone line out here a few months ago, and I don't want to have to sit out here all night waiting for the police to come." She frowned down at the man on the floor, who was covered in soup broth and sugar sprinkles. "Too bad you had to waste all that good food."

"Come by the diner sometime. You can have a meal on me." She phoned the sheriff's department.

10

MIX WELL

"Thank you so much for coming. It's so nice to have you here." Sammy greeted everyone as they came in the door of Sunny Cove Services. The opening party was turning out to be much larger than she could've imagined. Austin had been the first to sign up as a new employee, and several other people were waiting in line near the office door to do their paperwork, each one with a cookie in hand.

"I like this!" Austin exclaimed at her side.

"I do, too. Do you think you'll like working with other people?"

He bobbed his head. Austin had come a long way from the first time she'd met him, when he was just a scared young man running away from the cops because he'd been accused of stealing. More of his true personality showed every time she talked to him, and Sammy was so happy she was helping him out. "Uncle Mitch says he's really happy for me."

"Good. I have to talk to a few people. Are you all right for a minute?"

"I'm going to get another cookie!" Austin made a beeline for the food table.

Sonya McTavish slipped in the side door, dressed in a sleek black dress. She'd piled her hair on top of her head in a fancy updo, and she tapped Sammy on the shoulder. "Nice little party. It looks like you guys are going to be very good neighbors."

"I really hope so," Sammy said with a smile. "And I'm glad you're here. I wanted to ask you what it would cost to rent out one of the theaters sometime. Once we get a workforce, I'd like to treat them all to a movie."

Sonya flicked her long red fingernails in the air. "For you, absolutely nothing. I like what you're doing here, Sammy. We need more people like you in our community." She sauntered off to go talk to the mayor, who had just arrived with his wife.

A tug on her arm made her turn, and Sammy was

surprised to see Julia Richardson standing next to her. Just like Sonya, she'd come overdressed for the occasion in a pink skirt suit and tiny hat that looked like something right out of the Kennedy White House.

"Mrs. Richardson! I didn't expect you here!"

"And why not, dear? This was the last project my cousin Harold did, after all. I thought it was worth it to come and see, maybe as just my own little tribute to him. I'm glad to see it's actually finished, too."

Sammy didn't tell her about the trim pieces Mr. Lowry had finished nailing in. That could be her little secret if it made Julia feel better about Mr. Woodland. "It looks great, doesn't it?"

"It sure does. I have to admit I'm also here for the free cookies, and to tell you congratulations on the case." Mrs. Richardson gave her a knowing smile.

"What happened was purely accidental," she assured the other woman. "I just happened to be in the right place at the right time."

"Or the wrong place at the wrong time." Sheriff Jones loomed over the both of them now. Sammy hadn't even seen him arrive.

"I'll leave you two to talk." Julia winked at Sammy and scuttled over to the food table.

Sheriff Jones waited until she was gone before he said anything more. "I'm pretty sure I asked you to stay out of this."

"And I tried, sort of. I'd really just gone over there to give her my condolences. It was the right thing to do, especially since I was the one who'd found Harold and he'd been working for me when he died." She knew she didn't need to feel defensive about it. Some in the town were calling her a local hero, mostly prompted by Tracy Woodland who insisted that Sammy had saved her life. Sammy didn't want any of that kind of attention, but she hadn't really done anything wrong.

"That may be so, but you still put yourself in a very dangerous position."

"I suppose this all means that the paper in his pocket wasn't a suicide note after all?" she asked, trying to steer the conversation away from herself.

He took a deep breath and sighed. "No, it wasn't. It was probably more of an apology note. The two of them fought a lot, from what Mrs. Woodland told us. Harold would sometimes write her a note to say he was sorry, and they'd just had an argument before he left the house that morning."

She smiled a little as she thought of the grumpy contractor writing little notes to his wife. "That's good to know."

The sheriff's face was stern. "But you still shouldn't have gotten involved. I'm worried that one of these days you're going to get hurt. That's my job."

"What? To worry about me or to get hurt?"

He looked at her for a long moment before he answered. "Both, I suppose."

Sammy couldn't really argue with that. "Look, I really am sorry. I didn't mean to cause any trouble, and you have to admit that you also encouraged me to figure it all out. Otherwise, why sit there for an hour with me talking about the suspects?"

The tiniest of smiles changed his lips. "Yes, that must have been what it was." He cleared his throat. "I'm on duty, and I've got to get back to the station. But I did want to stop by and say congratulations. This is going to be really good for Austin and anyone else in his position. You're going to do great."

"Thanks."

Sheriff Jones left as Rob approached her. "Well, partner, what do you think? I'd say we actually did it." He looked around the room proudly.

"I wouldn't go talking too soon. I mean, we have yet to see how many people will want to come and work for us, and we have no idea how many people will be willing to use our services." The idea of giving meaningful jobs to the disabled was one that Sammy really liked, but she had no way of knowing if it would actually go over well. What if there weren't enough people in their area like Austin? What if they didn't get enough support from the community? The grant was enough to get them started, but they needed people to be sustainable.

"I don't think you need to worry about that. I just took a break from signing up new employees, and it looks like more are lining up." He nodded toward the office, where a young woman was passing out clipboards to everyone who had formed a line outside the door. "I brought in a candidate for manager that I think you're going to like, too. She's worked in social services before, and she had some very good references. Of course, I haven't officially given her the job, not without your approval, but I thought it would be good to invite her here and see how she does.

"So far, so good I'd say." Sammy felt warmth rush through her as she watched the woman talking to and interacting with the employment candidates. Sammy couldn't hear anything from her position on the other side of the room, and the crowd was also fairly noisy, but she could see by the looks on everyone's faces that they were getting along just fine.

"I also happen to know of a good-sized law firm that could use help with its document shredding," Rob added.

"That's very kind of you."

"It might look that way, but it's really just a good business decision. Why should I pay my current employees to stand at a shredder when their skills could be put to use elsewhere? It'll be very cost effective, and I don't think anyone will mind a little of the work being taken off their shoulders. I'm suggesting it to everyone I know. Considering that we're a non-profit, there shouldn't be any legal issues with that."

"You've thought of everything," Sammy replied. She excused herself to get a drink and found Helen near the cookie table. "What do you think?"

Her boss took a bite of a snickerdoodle. "I think you

must be a better woman than I am, considering you managed to teach Austin how to bake. Oh, honey, this is fabulous. You should have your picture in the paper."

"I already did, and it wasn't a flattering one," Sammy reminded her. The news van had shown up to Tracy Woodland's house in response to the shots fired, and they'd chosen to put a picture of a rather frazzled Sammy on the late night evening news. "I think it's better if I stay out of the news."

"And how about your new friend? Is she doing all right?" Helen was referring to Mrs. Woodland, who despite her cold attitude during the standoff had been very warm and thankful to Sammy ever since.

"She's coping really well, I think. She also volunteered to come in and teach our employees about secretarial skills like answering the phone and filling out paperwork. She said she wanted to find some way to contribute." It had all been a very strange string of events, but it was turning out nicely.

"I think you'll have more and more of that as you continue with this and people see what you're doing here," Helen said approvingly. "Good job, Sammy. Just like always."

"Thanks, Helen."

* * *

Thank you so much for reading, Cookies and Condolences. We hope you really enjoyed the story.

Also, make sure to sign up to receive PureRead Donna Doyle updates at PureRead.com for more great mysteries, exclusive offers and news of our new releases. We love to surprise our readers and would love to have you as part of our reader family!

Much love, and thanks again,

Your Friends at PureRead

* * *

Sign Up For Updates:
http://pureread.com/donnadoyle

BROWSE ALL OF DONNA DOYLE'S BOOKS
http://pureread.com/donnadoylebooks

Rainbow Mountain Brides Boxset

Mega Amish Romance Boxset

Christian Love 21 Book Contemporary Romance Boxset

** BROWSE ALL OF OUR BOX SETS **

http://PureRead.com/boxsets

ABOUT PUREREAD

Thank you for reading!

Here at PureRead we aim to serve you, our dear reader, with good, clean Christian stories. You can be assured that any PureRead book you pick up will not only be hugely enjoyable, but free of any objectionable content.

We are deeply thankful to you for choosing our books. Your support means that we can continue to provide stories just like the one you have just read.

PLEASE LEAVE A REVIEW

Please do consider leaving a review for this book on Amazon - something as simple as that can help others just like you discover and enjoy the books we publish, and your reviews are a constant encouragement to our hard working writers.

LIKE OUR PUREREAD FACEBOOK PAGE

Love Facebook? We do too and PureRead has a very special Facebook page where we keep in touch with readers.

To like and follow PureRead on Facebook go to **Facebook.com/pureread**

OUR WEBSITE

To browse all of our PureRead books visit our website at PureRead.com